Melodie
the Music
Fairy

by Daisy Meadows

illustrated by Georgie Ripper

ORCHARD BOOKS

www.rainbowmagic.co.uk

RAINBOW magic ®

The Party Fairies

For Alice and Lara Clerc, with the
hope that they will seek out and
find lovely fairies in France.

Special thanks to
Marilyn Kaye

ORCHARD BOOKS
96 Leonard Street, London EC2A 4XD
Hachette Children's Books
Level 17/207 Kent St, Sydney, NSW 2000
A Paperback Original
First published in Great Britain in 2004
Rainbow Magic is a registered trademark of Working Partners Limited.
Series created by Working Partners Limited, London W6 OQT
Text © Working Partners Limited 2004
Illustrations © Georgie Ripper 2004
The right of Georgie Ripper to be identified as the illustrator
of this work has been asserted by her in accordance
with the Copyright, Designs and Patents Act, 1988.
A CIP catalogue record for this book is available
from the British Library.
ISBN 1 84362 819 8
5 7 9 10 8 6
Printed in Great Britain

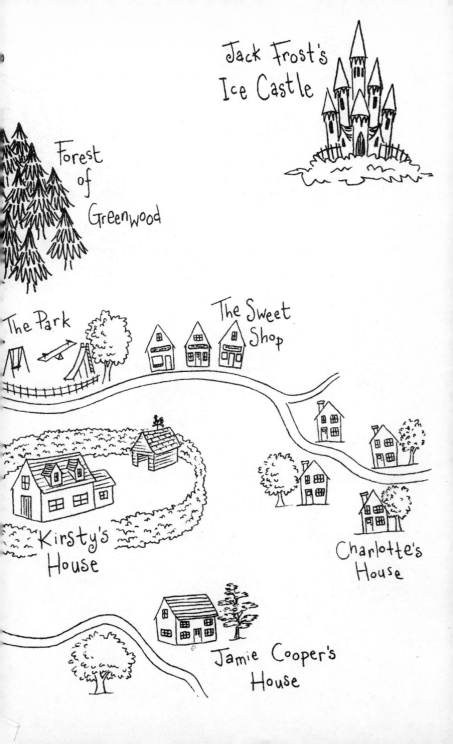

A Very Special Party Invitation

Our gracious King and gentle Queen
Are loved by fairies all.
One thousand years have they ruled well,
Through troubles great and small.

In honour of their glorious reign
A party has been planned,
To celebrate their jubilee
Throughout all Fairyland.

The party is a royal surprise,
We hope they'll be delighted.
So shine your wand and press your dress...
For you have been invited!

RSVP: HRH THE FAIRY GODMOTHER

Contents

Musical Mayhem

"Kirsty, you're a brilliant dancer!" Rachel Walker smiled, clapping her hands as her friend took a bow. Kirsty had just finished practising the ballet steps she would be performing later that evening.

"It will look even better tonight, with the other dancers and the proper costumes," Kirsty replied with a grin.

"And wait till you hear the lovely music."

Rachel was staying with her best friend, Kirsty Tate, for the week. That evening, the girls were going to the village hall for a special occasion – the first anniversary of Kirsty's ballet school.

"It's going to be a great party," Kirsty went on. "My ballet teacher is decorating the hall and organising some games, and all the parents are bringing food."

"It sounds fun," Rachel agreed. "But if it's a party, then we'll have to be on the lookout for goblins!"

Kirsty nodded. She and Rachel shared a magical secret: they were friends with the fairies! But, right now, there were problems in Fairyland and Kirsty and Rachel had promised to help.

The fairies were planning a surprise celebration for the 1000th jubilee of the Fairy King and Queen. It was meant to be taking place in five days' time, and the Party Fairies were in charge of making it as special as possible using their party bags of magic fairy dust.

But nasty Jack Frost had other plans. Banished to his ice castle by the Fairy King and Queen, he had decided to throw a party of his own on the very same day. Jack Frost knew that whenever a party in the human world went wrong, the Party Fairies would fly to the rescue.

So he had cunningly sent his goblin
servants to spoil as many human parties
as possible, and grab the fairies' party
bags when they flew in to set things
right. Then fairy magic would make his
party spectacular, but the jubilee
celebrations would be ruined!

Suddenly, the girls heard Mrs Tate's
voice. "Time to go, girls!" she called.

Kirsty and Rachel hurried downstairs
to join Kirsty's mum and dad.

Mr Tate held up a cake tin. "I made some cakes for the party," he explained, lifting the lid.

"Fairy cakes!" Rachel laughed with delight. "You couldn't have made anything better."

"Thanks, Dad," Kirsty grinned, tucking the tin under her arm.

Mr Tate drove them all to the village hall. They arrived to find it already full of friends and families who had come to join the celebration.

"The hall looks so different!" Kirsty gasped. Several rows of chairs had been set up to face the stage, just like in a real theatre.

Shiny silver streamers hung from the ceiling, twinkling fairy lights bordered the stage and bunches of silver and white balloons floated above each table of food.

While Mr and Mrs Tate chatted to
other parents, Rachel and Kirsty
arranged the fairy cakes on a plate.
The cakes weren't the
only things that
looked delicious.

"Yum, chocolate
éclairs!" Kirsty
pointed out.
Then she frowned.
"They look almost
too good to be true."

"Maybe we should
test some of these — just
to make sure the food
hasn't been spoiled by
a goblin," Rachel suggested.

Kirsty nodded. She took an éclair and
Rachel ate one of Mr Tate's fairy cakes.

Then the girls smiled at each other – the cakes were delicious, no goblins had been anywhere near this party food.

Just then, the ballet teacher, Miss Kelly, joined them. "Kirsty, it's time for you to go and get ready now," she said. "And you must be Rachel," she added with a smile. "Kirsty said you would be coming."

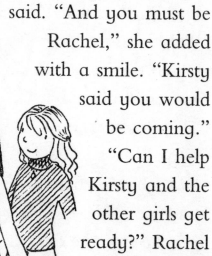

"Can I help Kirsty and the other girls get ready?" Rachel asked eagerly.

Miss Kelly nodded. "Thank you, Rachel. I could certainly use another pair of hands."

Kirsty led the way to the dressing room, which was behind the stage. While the dancers slipped into their tights and tutus, Rachel helped Miss Kelly apply rosy powder to the girls' cheeks and a dab of pink gloss to their lips. Finally, the dancers put on their ballet shoes, tying the pink satin ribbons firmly around their ankles.

There was a feeling of excitement in the air as the audience took their seats. Watching from backstage, Rachel breathed a sigh of relief. The decorations, the food and the costumes were perfect. It looked like Jack Frost's goblins hadn't heard about the ballet-school party.

Miss Kelly walked onto the stage. "Ladies and gentlemen, I am pleased to present our very first class of ballerinas, who will perform for you tonight in honour of our school's anniversary," she announced.

The audience clapped as Miss Kelly hurried into the wings. Then the curtain rose, and the music began.

With their arms held gracefully over their heads, the dancers ran daintily onto the stage. Having seen Kirsty practise, Rachel knew what was coming next. But she hadn't seen the dance with the costumes and music. She watched in delight – the girls looked as beautiful as fairies in their pretty, gauzy tutus.

But then, suddenly, the music changed. It seemed to speed up and the dancers started to have difficulty staying in time. Although they were dancing on bravely, Rachel could see from Kirsty's face that something was wrong.

She watched in dismay as one or two of the girls stumbled, stubbing their toes on the stage as they tried to pirouette more quickly.

The music was still getting faster and faster, and the tune was now just a squeaky jumble of noise. Rachel glanced across at Miss Kelly.

Red in the face, the teacher
was frantically pressing the
buttons on the CD-player,
one after the other, but
it wasn't making any
difference. The dancers
whirled and spun,
quicker and quicker, but it
was impossible for them to keep to the beat.
Two dancers bumped into each other, and
another tripped over her own feet.

"I can't stop the CD-player!" Miss Kelly
gasped. "I don't know what's wrong with it."

But Rachel knew. She was sure that this
was the work of one of Jack Frost's goblins!

The Trembling Tambourine

The girls abandoned their performance, and rushed offstage to see what was going on. A couple of the parents came too, to help Miss Kelly with the music. But nobody seemed to know what was wrong with the CD-player.

"This is definitely goblin mischief!" Rachel said to herself. She looked for

Kirsty, but couldn't see her in the crowd of people backstage. "Well, I'm going to find him and stop his tricks!"

Rachel glanced round the village hall, and her heart sank. She could see lots of places where a goblin could hide. Backstage there were trunks and racks of costumes and the big cardboard set from the last pantomime – not to mention two dressing rooms, a music room and a tiny office.

But then, just as Rachel was wondering where to start her search, she saw a pile of musical instruments stacked in the wings on the other side of the stage. And one of them, a tambourine, was shaking, all on its own!

Rachel gulped. She could see that there was no one on that side of the stage, and all the other instruments were still. She knew the tambourine was too small to hide a goblin, but what was making it tremble?

Could a goblin have brushed past it
and set it moving, she wondered.
And could the goblin still be lurking
over there?

As quietly as she could, Rachel slipped
across the stage to the other side. She
crept towards the stack of instruments,
looking around carefully in case the
goblin was hiding nearby.
She wanted to be sure
to spot him before
he spotted her!
But she couldn't
see anything
suspicious so, with
her heart pounding,
she knelt down beside the
tinkling tambourine. Very carefully,
Rachel lifted the rim with one finger.

As she did so, a golden glow flooded out from underneath.

Rachel grinned and lifted the tambourine away eagerly. She had already guessed what she would find, and sure enough, tucked away with her face buried in her gauzy skirt, was a tiny, shimmering fairy.

"You're a Party Fairy!" Rachel exclaimed with delight.

The fairy raised her head. She was sobbing so hard that she had been making the tambourine bells jingle.

Tears like tiny diamonds rolled down
her cheeks as she adjusted her little gold
hairband. "That's r-right, I'm Melodie
the Music Fairy," she sniffed sadly. "And
you must be Rachel."

Melodie stood up on tiptoe. She was
wearing a beautiful pink ballet dress, with
black musical notes all around the hem.
Her golden hair was in plaits that swung
as she turned her head.

"Where's Kirsty?" Melodie asked.

"She's not far away," Rachel told her. "But why are you crying?"

Melodie wiped away a last sparkling tear. "I came to fix the music," she explained. "If I had known one of those nasty goblins had made it go wrong, I would have been more careful."

Rachel frowned. "Was a goblin waiting for you?"

"Yes," Melodie wailed. "He grabbed my party bag and ran off with it. Now I can't fix the music for the girls' ballet. And if I don't get my party bag back, there won't be any music for the King and Queen's jubilee party, either!"

Melodie's Mission

Rachel felt very sorry for Melodie. "Don't worry," she said. "Kirsty and I will help you get your party bag back."

Melodie brightened immediately. "Oh, do you mean it?" she cried eagerly.

Rachel smiled. "Of course I do," she replied. "Now let's go and find Kirsty."

Quickly, Melodie picked up her glittering wand and fluttered into the pocket of Rachel's skirt. Then Rachel made her way back towards the people gathered around the CD-player.

Kirsty spotted her friend coming across the stage, and hurried to meet her. "Rachel, I think I know what happened to the music," Kirsty whispered in her ear. "It's goblin trouble!"

Rachel nodded. "Look!" she said, and held her skirt pocket open so Kirsty could peek inside.

Melodie waved at her. "Hello, Kirsty. I'm Melodie the Music Fairy," she called in her soft silvery voice.

"Oh, Melodie, I'm so pleased to see you," Kirsty said gratefully. "If anyone can help us, you can."

"She came here to fix the music," Rachel explained. "But a goblin stole her party bag."

Kirsty's face fell. "Oh, no!" she gasped. "We have to get it back before the goblin escapes and takes it to Jack Frost!"

Melodie nodded enthusiastically.
"But where should we start looking?"
she asked.

Rachel thought about this. "There are
so many people in the main hall, I
don't think he would hang around
there," she said. "Let's check the other
rooms backstage."

With all the noise and confusion, the

girls were able to slip away easily
without being noticed. They hurried
along the backstage corridor, and ran
into the ladies' dressing room. Rachel
looked in the lockers where the dancers
had left their clothes, while Kirsty
checked the cupboards and rummaged
through the costumes. There was no
sign of a goblin.

Next, they tried the office. Melodie
flew out of Rachel's pocket to look
under the desk, Rachel peered out of
the window, and Kirsty opened all the
drawers in the filing cabinet. There
were papers and folders everywhere, but
no goblin.

The three returned to
the corridor feeling a
little downhearted.

"Do you think
he's already
gone?" Rachel
asked glumly.

Melodie shook her
head, "Not with so many
people about," she replied. "He's hiding
somewhere until the coast is clear."

Suddenly Kirsty frowned. "I can hear
something!" she exclaimed, listening
hard. "Someone's playing the piano."

Now Rachel could hear it too, very
faintly. "Maybe someone is practising
in the music room," she suggested.

"But who would practise the piano
with a party going on?" asked Kirsty.

Rachel listened again. "Well,
whoever it is, they certainly need the
practice," she said, pulling a face.
"It sounds terrible!"

Melodie's face lit up. "Only a goblin
could play that badly!" she gasped, and
immediately she zoomed off towards
the sound. The girls ran after her.
As they got closer to the music room,
the jangling sound of the piano
grew louder.

They found the door ajar, and peeped cautiously into the room. They could hear the terrible music clearly now, and they could even see the piano standing in the middle of the floor. But to their astonishment, there was nobody playing it!

Goblin Discovered

The girls stared at the piano in amazement. Even Melodie looked puzzled. But then Kirsty had an idea. "Maybe the goblin's hiding inside the piano!" she said. "And playing it from there."

"Let's go and look," Rachel suggested.

"No, I'll go," Kirsty replied. "Ballet shoes are soft. If the goblin is in there, he won't hear me coming."

"Good idea," Rachel agreed.
If the goblin was hiding in
the piano, they didn't
want to give him
any warning.

Kirsty slipped
through the open
door and tiptoed
over to the grand
piano. Holding her
breath, she carefully
lifted the lid and
peeked inside.

And there he was – a
nasty-looking goblin, laughing
gleefully and running up and down
the piano strings, with Melodie's party
bag swinging from one knobbly hand.

As he pranced, he sang to himself in a croaky voice: "I've got the party bag, I'm such a smarty. I'll take it to Jack Frost, and he'll throw a party!" Ever so gently, Kirsty lowered the piano lid. Then she turned to the door and nodded at Rachel and Melodie. "What do we do now?" Rachel whispered to Melodie. "How are we going to get your party bag back?"

Melodie frowned thoughtfully, as Rachel looked around the room. There was a set of drums not far from the grand piano, and on one of the drums lay a pair of cymbals. This gave Rachel a clever idea. "See those cymbals?" she said, pointing them out to Melodie. "Do you think you could lift one?"

"I think so," Melodie replied, looking at Rachel curiously.

"Great! I'll take the other one," Rachel said.

"But how will you get there to pick it up?" Melodie asked. "If you walk across the room, the goblin might hear you."

"Not if I'm a fairy…" Rachel smiled.

Melodie nodded and waved her wand. A shower of glittering fairy dust floated down around Rachel and she felt herself shrinking. By the time the sparkling dust had settled, Rachel was as tiny as Melodie herself. She fluttered her wings happily and flew around in a little circle. Then she set off across the music room, with Melodie close behind.

The cymbals were heavy. Melodie
and Rachel both had
to struggle to lift
them, but at last
they managed it.

Quickly, they
flew over to
Kirsty, who had
been watching them in
bewilderment. Rachel whispered in
Kirsty's ear so the goblin wouldn't hear.

"When I wink, open the lid of the piano," she said.

Kirsty nodded, wondering what Rachel was planning.

Rachel and Melodie held up the cymbals and hovered in the air, face to face. Then Rachel winked at Kirsty who immediately lifted the piano lid. At the very same moment, Rachel and Melodie rushed towards each other. And with a crash that shook the room, the cymbals clashed together right above the goblin's head!

A New Problem

The goblin let out a loud scream, clapped his hands over his ears and dropped Melodie's party bag. "Oh, what a dreadful noise!" he shrieked in surprise. "My poor head hurts!" And he leapt out of the piano and ran from the room at top speed.

Rachel smiled to herself. The cymbals had made a deafening noise, she thought, but at least she and Melodie had been ready for it. She heard a smaller crash, and looked round to see that Melodie had dropped her cymbal and swooped into the piano to snatch up her party bag.

"Ooh, that was fun!" Melodie exclaimed. "The goblin escaped, but I've got my party bag and that's all that matters." She opened the bag and peeped inside. As she did so, some glittering, golden musical notes drifted out. "And it's still full of magic fairy dust," she declared happily.

At that moment, Kirsty heard footsteps in the corridor outside. "Someone's coming," she whispered. "Quick, you two, hide in the piano!"

Rachel dropped her cymbal with a clatter and flew to join Melodie inside the piano. Kirsty let the lid down quickly. She was just in time. The door to the room swung open, and Miss Kelly came in. "Hello, Kirsty, are you all right?" she asked anxiously. "Whatever was all that noise?"

Kirsty had to think very quickly.

"Er, I thought that there, um, might be another CD-player in this room," she explained. "I was looking for it when I knocked over the cymbals."

Miss Kelly laughed. "Well, we need you on stage now. I think we'll be able to start the ballet again in a minute. Melissa's dad is an electrician, and he's fixing the CD-player."

Kirsty frowned. Could a human electrician fix a machine that was broken by a goblin? She had a feeling that only fairy magic would get that CD-player working again. And she knew just who could help. But Melodie was stuck inside the piano with Rachel!

"I'll come in a moment, Miss Kelly," Kirsty said, thinking fast. "Some sequins fell off my costume. I just need to find them first."

"Your costume looks fine," the ballet teacher told her briskly. "A sequin or two makes no difference. Besides, there's no time to sew them back on, and we don't want to keep our audience waiting any longer."

Kirsty had no choice. Reluctantly, she followed Miss Kelly out of the music room, leaving Rachel and Melodie trapped inside the piano.

The Show Must Go On!

"Oh, no!" Rachel cried after Kirsty and Miss Kelly had gone. "Who knows how long we're going to be stuck in here now?"

Melodie laughed, a tinkling musical sound. "Don't worry, Rachel," she said. And with a wave of her magic wand, the piano lid flew open in a shower of sparkling fairy magic.

Rachel and Melodie flew out. As soon as Rachel reached the ground, Melodie waved her wand again and turned Rachel back to her normal size. Then, clutching her party bag tightly, Melodie hid herself in Rachel's pocket. "We can save the party now," she said happily. "Let's go!"

As Rachel hurried out of the music room, she noticed that the squeaky, speeded-up music had stopped. She wondered if the spell had been broken when the goblin ran away. Or maybe Melissa's dad had fixed the CD-player somehow.

When she reached the stage, however, she saw a large group of people still gathered around the machine. Peering through the crowd, Rachel caught a glimpse of Melissa's dad with a screwdriver in one hand and a pair of pliers in the other. Miss Kelly and Kirsty were by his side.

"What's happening?" Melodie hissed from Rachel's pocket.

"I think Melissa's dad took the CD-player apart," Rachel whispered.

"There are bits of metal and plastic all over the floor."

"Is he going to put it back together now?" Melodie wanted to know.

"I think so," Rachel murmured. She edged a little closer.

"I'm terribly sorry," the man was saying to Miss Kelly. "I've repaired CD-players before, but I've never seen anything like this. I don't think I can fix it."

"Do you think *you* can fix it?" Rachel whispered to Melodie.

"Yes, I'm sure I can – with fairy magic," Melodie answered. She peeped out of Rachel's pocket and her face fell. "But not with all these people around," she added. "Someone would see me sprinkling fairy dust over the machine."

"Maybe I can get everyone to move away," Rachel said thoughtfully. But though she racked her brains, she couldn't think of anything that would make the people leave the CD-player.

She looked round, hoping that a
brilliant notion would pop into her
head. And then she remembered the
musical instruments in the wings on the
other side of the stage, where she had
first found Melodie.

They couldn't be seen from the
CD-player, but when Rachel slipped
across to the pile of instruments, she
was pleased to see that there was
nobody else about.

Gently, she lifted the little fairy out of her pocket. "Look," she said softly. "I've got an idea. Can you do anything with these musical instruments instead?"

Melodie smiled and clapped her hands.

"Yes, I can!" she exclaimed. "Is anyone looking?"

"No, we're out of sight round here," Rachel told her.

Quickly, Melodie fluttered over to the instruments and perched lightly on the violin. She took a handful of glittering musical notes from her party bag, and carefully sprinkled them over the violin's strings.

Then she flitted from instrument to instrument, throwing a few sparkling notes over each one. Finally, she waved her wand with an expert flourish.

At once, the bow that had been lying next to the violin floated into the air and began stroking the violin's strings.

The flute hovered, quivering, as soft, sweet sounds poured from it, while the strings of a harp were plucked by invisible fingers. Rachel heard the deep, low notes of a horn and watched in amazement as all the instruments began to play themselves.

From across the stage, Rachel heard
Miss Kelly exclaim in surprise. "That's
our ballet music!" she cried. "Where is
it coming from?"

Rachel ran back to the group. "I
found another CD-player," she told the
ballet teacher. She caught Kirsty's eye
and smiled. Rachel didn't have to tell
her friend that there was fairy magic
at work!

"Quickly, dancers take your places," Miss Kelly called. As the girls rushed onto the stage, the audience moved back to their seats.

Miss Kelly turned to Rachel. "Could you start the music from the beginning again, please?" she asked.

Rachel bit her lip. She wasn't sure that she could. What if Melodie had already gone back to Fairyland? Anxiously, she hurried back to the instruments, and then she smiled with relief. She should have known that Melodie wouldn't leave without saying goodbye.

The fairy was still there, dancing around to the music, her white dress swirling around her.

"Can you start the music from the beginning?" Rachel asked her.

Melodie's wand fluttered and she threw a few more glittering musical notes into the air. The music stopped for an instant, and then began all over again.

As Kirsty and the others began to dance, Rachel and Melodie watched the performance from the wings. "Oh, it's lovely!" Melodie exclaimed, copying the dancers' graceful arm movements.

"Just like it should be," Rachel agreed.

The ballet went perfectly, and at the end the audience applauded wildly. The girls curtseyed, left the stage and went to join their proud parents. Except for Kirsty, who rushed over to the side of the stage.

"Thank you, Melodie," she said gratefully. "You saved our party."

"No, thank you," Melodie beamed. "Without you, there would be no music at the King and Queen's jubilee. Please keep an eye out for any more of Jack Frost's goblins."

"We will," Rachel and Kirsty promised together.

Melodie beamed. "Good luck," she said, and with a wave of her wand and a shower of twinkling lights, the fairy flew away.

Smiling happily, Rachel and Kirsty made their way to the hall to enjoy the rest of the party.

"I hope we meet more Party Fairies," Rachel said.

"Oh, I'm sure we will," replied Kirsty, and then she smiled. "As long as we keep going to parties!" she added.

The Party Fairies

Cherry and Melodie have their magic
party bags back. Now Rachel
and Kirsty must help

Grace the Glitter Fairy

Win a Rainbow Magic
Sparkly T-Shirt and Goody Bag!

In every book in the Rainbow Magic Party Fairies series (books 15-21) there is a hidden picture of a magic party bag with a secret letter in it. Find all seven letters and re-arrange them to make a special Fairyland word, then send it to us. Each month we will put the entries into a draw and select one winner to receive a Rainbow Magic Sparkly T-shirt and Goody Bag!

Send your entry on a postcard to Rainbow Magic Competition, Orchard Books, 96 Leonard Street, London EC2A 4XD. Australian readers should write to Level 17/207 Kent St, Sydney, NSW 2000. Don't forget to include your name and address. Only one entry per child. Final draw: 28th April 2006.

Coming Soon...
The Jewel Fairies

INDIA THE MOONSTONE FAIRY
1-84362-958-5

SCARLETT THE GARNET FAIRY   1-84362-954-2

EMILY THE EMERALD FAIRY   1-84362-955-0

CHLOE THE TOPAZ FAIRY
1-84362-956-9

AMY THE AMETHYST FAIRY
1-84362-957-7

SOPHIE THE SAPPHIRE FAIRY
1-84362-953-4

LUCY THE DIAMOND FAIRY
1-84362-959-3

Also coming soon . . .

SUMMER THE HOLIDAY FAIRY

1-84362-638-1

Summer the Holiday Fairy is getting all hot and
bothered, trying to keep Rainspell Island the best
place to go on vacation. Jack Frost has stolen the
sand from the beaches, and three magical shells.
The fairies need Rachel and Kirsty's help
to get the holiday magic back...

Have you checked out the

Website at:
www.rainbowmagic.co.uk

There are games, activities and
fun things to do, as well as news
and information about Rainbow
Magic and all of the fairies.

RAINBOW magic

by Daisy Meadows

Ruby the Red Fairy	ISBN	1 84362 016 2
Amber the Orange Fairy	ISBN	1 84362 017 0
Saffron the Yellow Fairy	ISBN	1 84362 018 9
Fern the Green Fairy	ISBN	1 84362 019 7
Sky the Blue Fairy	ISBN	1 84362 020 0
Izzy the Indigo Fairy	ISBN	1 84362 021 9
Heather the Violet Fairy	ISBN	1 84362 022 7

The Weather Fairies

Crystal the Snow Fairy	ISBN	1 84362 633 0
Abigail the Breeze Fairy	ISBN	1 84362 634 9
Pearl the Cloud Fairy	ISBN	1 84362 635 7
Goldie the Sunshine Fairy	ISBN	1 84362 641 1
Evie the Mist Fairy	ISBN	1 84362 636 5
Storm the Lightning Fairy	ISBN	1 84362 637 3
Hayley the Rain Fairy	ISBN	1 84362 638 1

The Party Fairies

Cherry the Cake Fairy	ISBN	1 84362 818 X
Melodie the Music Fairy	ISBN	1 84362 819 8
Grace the Glitter Fairy	ISBN	1 84362 820 1
Honey the Sweet Fairy	ISBN	1 84362 821 X
Polly the Party Fun Fairy	ISBN	1 84362 822 8
Phoebe the Fashion Fairy	ISBN	1 84362 823 6
Jasmine the Present Fairy	ISBN	1 84362 824 4
Holly the Christmas Fairy	ISBN	1 84362 661 6

All priced at £3.99. Holly the Christmas Fairy priced at £4.99.
Rainbow Magic books are available from all good bookshops, or can be ordered
direct from the publisher: Orchard Books, PO BOX 29, Douglas IM99 1BQ
Credit card orders please telephone 01624 836000
or fax 01624 837033 or visit our Internet site: www.wattspub.co.uk
or e-mail: bookshop@enterprise.net for details.

To order please quote title, author and ISBN and your full name and address.
Cheques and postal orders should be made payable to 'Bookpost plc.'
Postage and packing is FREE within the UK
(overseas customers should add £2.00 per book).
Prices and availability are subject to change.